Habitat Spy

Cynthia Kieber-King
Christina Wald

Let's spy in the forest . . .
hemlocks stand,
millipedes hide,
owls rest,
deer stride.

Let's spy on the mountain . . .
lichens cling,
midges dance,
eagles rise,
sheep prance.

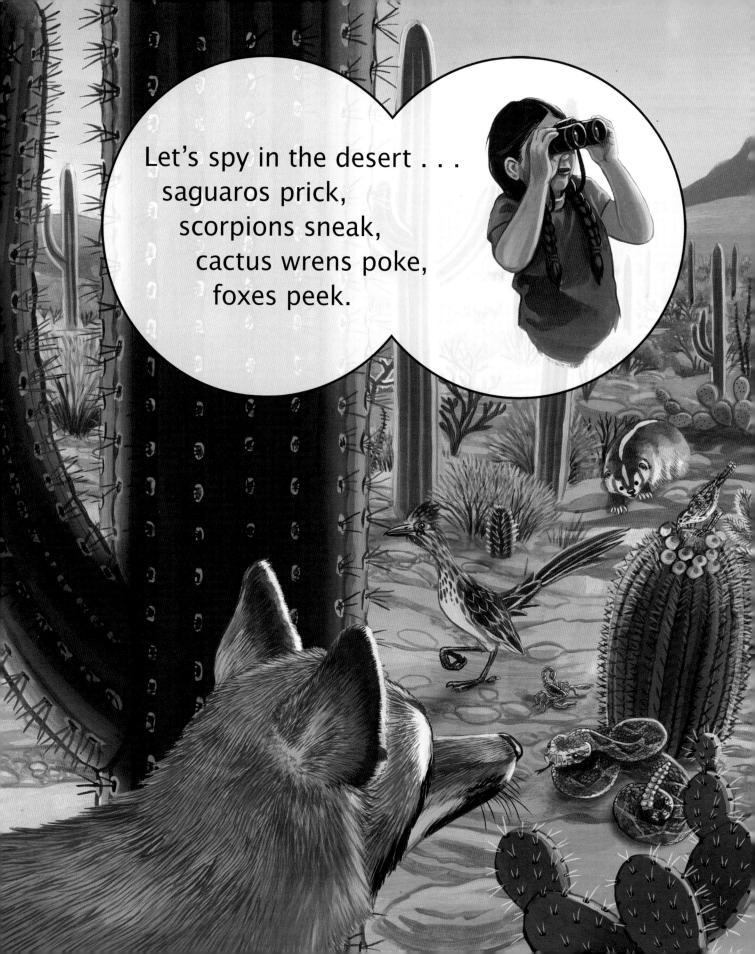

For Creative Minds

What is in a Habitat?

Habitats are more than just the plants and animals that live there. They are communities of plants, animals and non-living things that interact in certain locations. Look at the illustrations for the different habitats in the book and see if you can figure out some of the answers to the following habitat questions. For possible answers and a list of all of the plants and animals in each of the habitat illustrations, go to www.SylvanDellPublishing.com, click on the book's cover, and then the Teaching Activities.

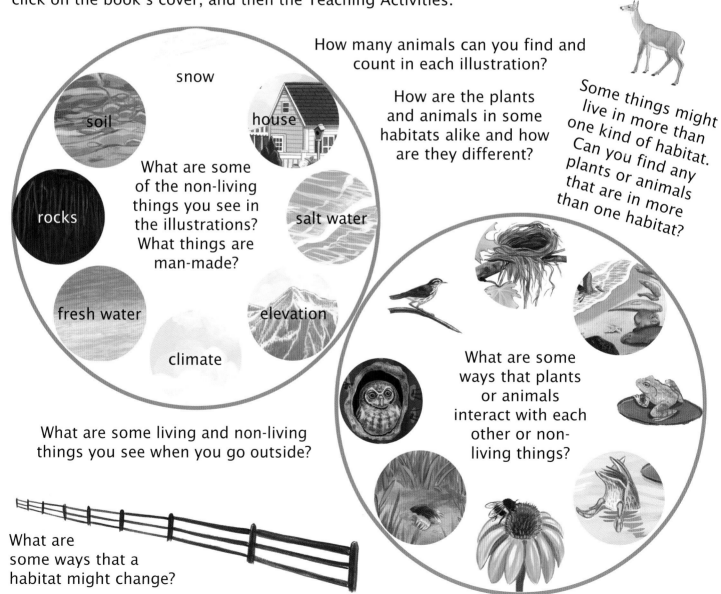

snow

soil

house

rocks

salt water

What are some of the non-living things you see in the illustrations? What things are man-made?

fresh water

elevation

climate

How many animals can you find and count in each illustration?

How are the plants and animals in some habitats alike and how are they different?

Some things might live in more than one kind of habitat. Can you find any plants or animals that are in more than one habitat?

What are some ways that plants or animals interact with each other or non-living things?

What are some living and non-living things you see when you go outside?

What are some ways that a habitat might change?

Adaptations and Basic Needs: True or False Questions

Plants and animals (living things) live in habitats that meet all of their basic needs. Animals need food, water, oxygen to breathe, and a safe space for shelter and to give birth to their young. Plants need sunlight and heat (temperature), water, soil to grow, and a way for seeds to move (disperse).

Living things have body parts and behaviors (adaptations) that help them live in their habitats and meet their basic needs. Can you tell if the statements are true or false?

1 Animals need oxygen to breathe. Many mammals take in oxygen through their mouths or noses, fish use gills, and some marine mammals (dolphins and whales) come to the surface of the water and take oxygen in using blowholes.

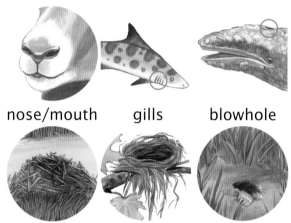

nose/mouth   gills   blowhole

2 All animals raise their young in burrows, nests, or dens.

beaver lodge   bird nest   digging mole

3 Living things have body parts or behaviors to protect themselves from predators or things that might hurt them.

spray   spines   school

4 Most animals move from one place to another. Special body parts help them move in their habitat but not easily in other habitats. For example, which body parts help animals move in the air, land, or water?

fluke   wings   legs & feet

5 All living things need energy to grow and have body parts to help them get food.

green leaves   talons   beak/mouth

Food Chains and Webs: The Circle of Life

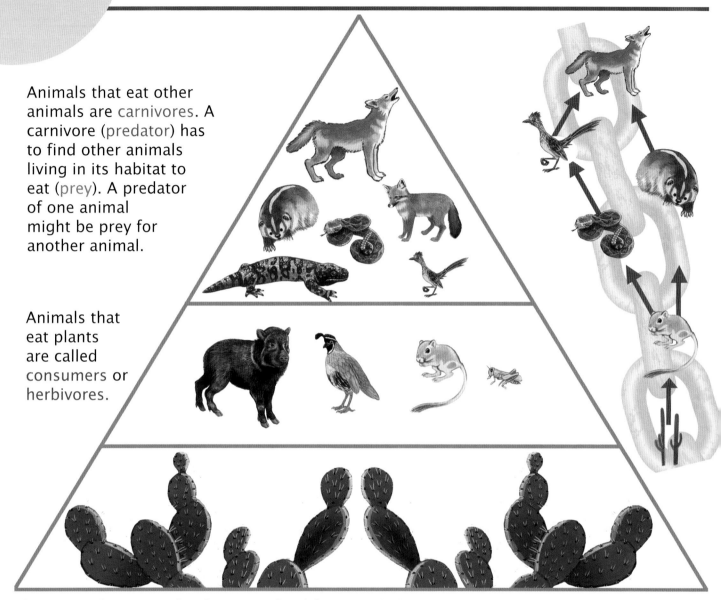

Animals that eat other animals are carnivores. A carnivore (predator) has to find other animals living in its habitat to eat (prey). A predator of one animal might be prey for another animal.

Animals that eat plants are called consumers or herbivores.

Plants (producers) make their own food from sunlight (photosynthesis) and nutrients in the soil that come from decaying things that were once alive.

Omnivores eat both plants and animals.

All of the plants and animals that are eaten by or that eat a particular animal are part of that animal's food chain. One habitat will have many different food chains that are linked together, called a food web.

Food for thought: Some animals live in more than one habitat. For example, a cougar (also called mountain lion, puma, or panther) and bighorn sheep might live in the desert and mountains.

- Could you find animals that live in a swamp in the desert? Why or why not?
- Could you find animals that live in a cave in the desert? Why or why not?

Odd One Out: Classification and Habitats

Which item is different from the rest? Answers are upside down on the bottom of the page.

Plants are at the bottom of food webs. Which one is not a plant?

All **birds** have feathers and wings but not all birds fly. Which one of these is not a bird, but a flying mammal?

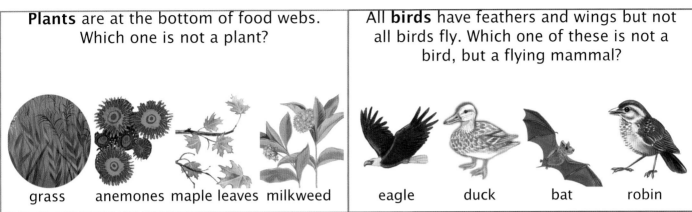

grass   anemones   maple leaves   milkweed   eagle   duck   bat   robin

Invertebrates don't have a backbone (vertebrate) at any stage of their lives. They live in all habitats, even deep in the ocean. Which of these is not an invertebrate?

All **mammal** babies drink milk from their mothers and get their oxygen from the air. Which of these mammals lives in the ocean?

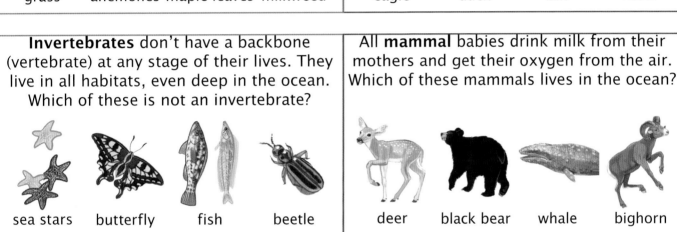

sea stars   butterfly   fish   beetle   deer   black bear   whale   bighorn

Which of these living things would not survive living in water or **wetlands**?

Which of these animals would you not find living in a **forest**?

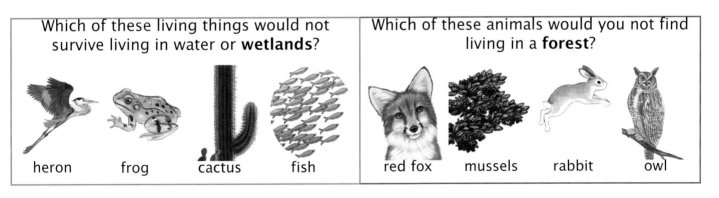

heron   frog   cactus   fish   red fox   mussels   rabbit   owl

Answers: **Plants**: Sea anemones are animals (invertebrates), not a plant. **Birds**: Bats are the only mammals that fly. **Invertebrates**: Fish have backbones (vertebrates). Some scientists worry that animal names like starfish or jellyfish are confusing because those animals are not fish. They recommend using "sea star" or "jellies" instead. Insects, beetles, and mollusks are all types of invertebrates. **Mammals**: Whales and dolphins are marine mammals. They come to the surface of the water to breathe through blowholes. **Wetlands**: The heron, frog, and fish live in or around water but the cactus can only live in dry habitats. **Forest**: Mussels need saltwater to live.

Thanks to Eliza Russell, Director of Education at the National Wildlife Federation, for verifying the information in this book.

For my son Justin and husband Dave, who happily explore all kinds of wonderful habitats with me. I'm grateful for your love and support—CKK

To mom for all her support and encouragement over the years—CW

Publisher's Cataloging-In-Publication Data

Kieber-King, Cynthia.
   Habitat spy / Cynthia Kieber-King ; [illustrated by] Christina Wald.
   p. : col. ill. ; cm.
   Summary: In rhyming narrative, readers are invited to find plants, invertebrates, birds and mammals living in thirteen different North American habitats. Includes "For Creative Minds" educational section.
   Issued also as pdf reproduction in English and pdf translation in Spanish, as well as eBook featuring auto-flip, auto-read, 3D-page-curling, and selectable English and Spanish text and audio
   ISBN: 978-1-60718-122-4 (hardcover)
   ISBN: 978-1-60718-132-3 (pbk.)
   ISBN: 978-1-60718-142-2 (English ebook)
   ISBN: 978-1-60718-152-1 (Spanish ebook)

   1. Habitat (Ecology)--North America--Juvenile literature. 2. Ecology--North America--Juvenile literature. 3. Habitat (Ecology)--North America. 4. Ecology--North America. I. Wald, Christina. II. Title.
QH541.14 .K54 2011
577.097   2010941279

Manufactured in China, January, 2011
This product conforms to CPSIA 2008
First Printing

Sylvan Dell Publishing
612 Johnnie Dodds, Suite A2
Mt. Pleasant, SC 29464

Interest level: 004-008
Grade level: P-3
ATOS™ Level: 3.7
Lexile Level: 1310 Lexile Code: AD

Curriculum keywords: adaptations, basic needs, classification (plants, invertebrates, birds, mammals), food webs, habitats, living/non-living